# Einstein —
# Champion
# of the World

## ALAN TRUSSELL-CULLEN

illustrated by Lorenzo Van Der Lingen

Learning Media

# Chapter 1

Most cats are pretty smart – that's why people say cats have nine lives. Whenever they get into trouble, cats usually find a way to save themselves.

But our cat Einstein is different. Dad says that Einstein doesn't have a brain at all because he can't work out simple things like "up" and "down." (He's very good at climbing *up* a tree but not so good at getting down again.)

The fire brigade has been to our house five times to get Einstein down from trees! Last time, the fire chief was so mad that he wagged his finger at Dad. He said that next time they'll turn the hose on him! (I think they meant the cat, not Dad.)

Of course, we all love Einstein just the same. But, being a cat with very little brain, at times he needs a lot of looking after. This is the story of one of those times. It all began when our new neighbors moved in.

# Chapter 2

Before I tell you about our new neighbors, I have to tell you one more thing about Einstein. Most cats have places where they like to sit and play and climb. They don't like other cats coming into these special places.

But not Einstein. If a cat comes snarling and growling onto his patch, he always uses the same secret plan – *he runs away!* If the other cat wants a good fight, Einstein uses his very secret weapon – *he climbs something!* Usually it's a lamp post or a tree (or even a person if they're nearby).

So, the other cats in our street walk through our yard whenever they want to. Einstein just gives them a goofy look as they curl up on his favorite blanket or finish the food in his bowl.

But at least it keeps Einstein out of fights. Well, it did, until the day the Stefani family moved in next door. First came the van with all the furniture. Then came the Stefanis – Mr. and Mrs. Stefani and their daughter, Gemma. And finally, the Stefani pets arrived.

Mom sticks by the "one pet" rule, but the Stefanis have three pets, and they all have weird names – a rabbit called Christmas Dinner, a parrot called Bird Brain, and a cat called Napoleon.

And then there's Gemma, but she's not a pet! Far from it. To start with, she's a girl, and if that's not bad enough, she's the same age as me. Even worse, she's in my class! So, now Mom always knows if I have homework – she just asks Gemma. It's made my life very difficult! But things were a thousand times worse for Einstein.

# Chapter 3

It all started like this. One day, not long after the Stefanis moved in, I was watching TV with Grandpa. It was his favorite show, *Boxing Stars in the Big Ring*. We always sit on the sofa and eat pretzels and shout and cheer. Mom doesn't like this. She says Grandpa gets too excited and that one day he'll have a heart attack. But there he was, bouncing up and down and shouting, "Come on, Swinger Samson!"

Suddenly, there was a terrifying noise. It started as a squeal and then turned into a squawk that went on and on like a fire alarm. We both ran to the window and gasped. Einstein was halfway up the lamp post outside our house. Down below was our new neighbors' cat, Napoleon. *He* was making the terrible yowling noises.

Grandpa was furious. He ran outside with his walking stick and swung at Napoleon. "Off you go, you nasty cat!" he yelled. But Napoleon ducked, snarled, and then trotted slowly away. With a flick of his tail, he jumped over the fence into his own place.

Einstein was still stuck halfway up the pole. It was his old up and down problem. Grandpa had to get Dad's rickety old ladder and hold it while Mom climbed up to rescue Einstein. "One day this stupid ladder is going to fall to pieces!" Mom grumbled.

That was Einstein's first battle with
Napoleon – and it wasn't the last. In fact,
Napoleon became the ruler of the whole
street. He chased *every* cat in *every*
direction. But the cat he picked on the
most was Einstein. Poor old Einstein tried
all his usual tricks, but Napoleon could
walk, run, and climb faster!

Grandpa even tried to give Einstein some boxing lessons, but that only made things worse. When Napoleon had finished "boxing" with Einstein, we had to take our poor cat to the vet. The vet was really getting to know Einstein.

# Chapter 4

Things really went wild on the day of the barbecue. Mom was having a barbecue for our new neighbors so they could meet everyone in the street. Dad was delighted because he was going through a cooking craze. Dad is always having crazes. Once it was origami. Every mealtime, he made origami animals with the napkins.

But now the craze was cooking. He had borrowed a Mexican cookbook from the library. "I'll barbecue some steak and some sausages," he said, "and I'll make some delicious chili pepper salsa to go with them." Little did he know the trouble his cooking would cause.

When people started to arrive, Dad took the steak out to the barbecue and got ready to cook it. He left the sausages in the fridge for later. Einstein knew that something important was happening, so he decided to help by getting in everyone's way. I could see that he was going to get into trouble, so I carried him into the kitchen. That was a mistake.

Mom came back into the kitchen to get
some milk, and while she poured it into a
jug, she left the fridge door open. Einstein
saw the pile of sausages and jumped in to
investigate. Mom kicked the door shut, and
Einstein was trapped inside! Mom had no
idea!

Meanwhile, Dad was mixing up his "secret recipe." Mom kept frowning and saying, "Do you think you need some help with that?"

Dad said gruffly, "Of course not! Anyone can follow a recipe, especially a great chef like me!" So there he was, counting out the chilies. "Only half a chili pepper?" he muttered. "That can't be right. They must mean half a cupful!"

All of the neighbors had arrived for the barbecue. "Are you sure everything's ready?" asked Mom.

"Of course!" said Dad, with a happy smile. "Everything's under control!"

Now, Dad's idea of a barbecue is simple.
He turns the gas up to full until the
barbecue is red hot! Then he throws on the
steaks. Then he starts talking to someone
and completely forgets he's doing the
cooking … until he smells the smoke. And
that's exactly what happened this time!

"Never mind," said Dad, looking at the black steaks. "We'll give them to Einstein."

"He won't eat them," said Mom. "They're burned!"

"I'll put some of my salsa on them," he said. "He'll never know the difference!"

"But what will we eat?" asked Mom.

"Sausages!" said Dad. "I bought a stack of them. Now, where is that dumb cat?" *That* was a very good question!

# Chapter 5

All afternoon, Napoleon had been watching our place through a hole in the fence. He'd seen the steaks and smelled the cooking meat. He'd seen Dad put the steaks into Einstein's bowl and pour something special over them (probably a tasty sauce, he thought). As soon as Dad went inside to get the sausages, Napoleon crept up the back steps to enjoy Einstein's dinner.

But what about Einstein? How do you keep warm inside a fridge? Even a pea-brained furball like Einstein feels the cold after a while. Well, explorers will tell you that one way to keep yourself warm is to eat! And that's exactly what Einstein had been doing. He'd been eating *lots* of sausages.

The next thing everyone heard was Dad's howl of rage! "Out!" he yelled. "Out of that fridge! Out of this house! Out of this planet before I …" For once, Einstein knew exactly what Dad was saying. He ran for the back door like a flash … just in time to meet Napoleon with his first mouthful of steak and Dad's chili salsa.*

*This was his mistake — big time! You see, Dad had been wrong about the salsa — it was half a chili pepper, not half a cupful! This salsa was ultrahot! Megahot! Raging inferno hot!

Napoleon was bowled over by Einstein the
furry cannonball, and the two cats rolled
down the steps. Napoleon was stunned!
Einstein the wimp was now Einstein the
monster! And what was happening inside
Napoleon's mouth? His insides were on fire!

Then Napoleon did the unthinkable! He
turned and ran away from Einstein! He not
only ran away, he was so terrified that he
shot straight up the first tree he came to,
right in the middle of our yard!

Mrs. Stefani saw Napoleon run up the tree. She saw Dad waving his arms and shouting like he was crazy. She thought that Dad was going to do something horrible to her poor cat!

"No, no!" said Dad. "I can explain everything!"

"I don't want an explanation," said Mrs. Stefani. "I want my cat!"

"I'll have him down in no time!" said Dad as he ran to get his ladder.

"Careful!" called Mom as Dad climbed up the ladder. But her warning came too late. Napoleon didn't like the look of this strange creature creeping up on him. He suddenly raced down the tree, down Dad, and down the ladder! In two blinks of an eye, Napoleon was over the fence and home.

Dad got such a fright that he pushed out
with his legs, and his rickety ladder finally
fell to pieces. It crashed to the ground,
leaving him hanging with his legs dangling.

"Help!" he cried.

"I'll get the fire brigade," said Mom.

"Oh, no," moaned Dad. "Not the fire
brigade!" He was remembering the fire
chief's warning.

# Chapter 6

It took the fire brigade only five minutes to arrive. The fire chief couldn't wait to see Dad swinging from the tree. He laughed and laughed.

"Get me down," said Dad. "Please!"

When Dad was safely on the ground, everyone cheered. Then the fire chief picked up a piece of Dad's ladder and said, "I'm glad you don't work for the fire brigade!"

Mom phoned up and had some pizzas delivered (and quietly threw away Dad's salsa). The fire chief said they were having a quiet day, so he let the crew stay for pizza and fruit punch. It turned into quite a party.

And what happened to Einstein after all this fuss? Well, Napoleon must have had the fright of his life because he never came anywhere near our yard again. Grandpa was very proud of Einstein. He said it was a wonderful plan to hide in the fridge and take nasty old Napoleon by surprise. In fact, he called Einstein the Champion of the World. "Better than Swinger Samson!" he said.

The Stefanis are talking to us again. In fact, everything is nearly back to normal. But there's one thing Mom and Dad don't know about yet. We're going to be a two-pet family very soon. You see, Gemma's rabbit, Christmas Dinner, is going to have babies, and Gemma says I can have one! I haven't told Mom yet, but I'm sure she won't mind.

I'm sure Einstein won't mind either – now that he's Champion of the World! (Well, the champion of our street at least!)